BEDTIME STORIES

THE EMPEROR'S NEW CLOTHES

GOLDILOCKS AND THE THREE BEARS

THE LITTLE PINK ROSE

THE PRINCESS AND THE PEA

HANS IN LUCK

THE WALRUS AND THE CARPENTER

THE OWL AND THE PUSSYCAT

BED IN SUMMER

"If you want your children to be intelligent, read them fairy tales.
If you want them to be more intelligent, read them more fairy tales."

– Albert Einstein

To our mother, who wanted us all to be intelligent.

DESIGNED BY
STEPHANIE MEYERS

THE EMPEROR'S NEW CLOTHES

Tany years ago there lived an Emperor who laid so great a value upon new clothes that he spent all his money on them in order to be smartly dressed. He did not care in the least about his soldiers, took no pleasure in theatre going, nor found a liking to drive into the wood, unless he could show off his new clothes. He had a robe for every hour of the day.

There was a merry life in the town where he lived. Plenty of strangers arrived daily, and one day there also came two swindlers. They pretended to be weavers, claiming they knew how to weave the finest fabrics imaginable. Not only, they asserted, were the colors and patterns uncommonly fine, but the clothes, made of this stuff, would have the amazing quality to become invisible to any person who was either unfit for the office he holds, or unpardonably stupid.

"Those would indeed be splendid clothes," thought the Emperor. "By possessing them I should be able to find out which men in my realm are unfit for the position they occupy, and thus I could distinguish the wise men from the fools. Yes, no doubt. I must give them orders for that fabric to be woven for me at once!" He handed the two swindlers a large fortune that they should set to work.

They put up two looms, and pretended to work, but they had nothing at all on the loom. Nevertheless, they called for the finest silk and the purest gold thread. But all this they put into their own bags working on the empty looms till late at night.

"Now, I wonder how they are getting on with their weaving," thought the Emperor. But he was quite uncomfortable at the idea that no one might be able to see it.

"I will send my old loyal minister to the weavers," thought the Emperor. "He can best judge how the cloth looks, for he is clever, and no one fills his post better than he does!"

So the good, old minister went into the room where the two impostors sat working at the empty looms.

"God bless me!"
thought the old minister, opening his eyes wide.
"In truth! I can't see anything!"
But, being a cautious man, he said nothing.

Both the swindlers begged him to step nearer, asking him if the patterns were not very pretty and the coloring beautiful.

Thereupon, they pointed to the empty loom, and the poor, old minister kept opening his eyes wide, but he was unable to see anything because there was nothing to see.

"Goodness me!" thought he.
"Can it really be that I am so dull? I have never thought so, and nobody must know it! Am I not fit for my office? No, it won't do to tell that I cannot see the stuff."

"Well, Sir, you don't say anything about it?" asked one of the weavers.

"Oh, it is so nice, most charming!" answered the old minister, peeping through his spectacles. "What a pattern and these colors! Yes, I am going to tell the Emperor that both please me very much!"

"Well, we are glad to hear that," said the two weavers, and then they named the colors and explained the strange pattern. The old minister paid great attention to everything, that he might be able to repeat it to the Emperor on his return. And so he did.

Now the swindlers demanded still more money, more silk, and more gold for weaving. They put all into their own pockets, and not a bit of thread was put at the empty looms.

The Emperor presently sent again another able official to learn how the weaving was proceeding and if the stuff would soon be ready. But he fared just as the first one. He gazed and gazed, but as, apart from the empty loom, there was nothing visible. He could not see anything else.

"Is this not a pretty piece of stuff?" asked both the swindlers, showing and explaining the magnificent pattern that did not exist at all.

"Stupid, certainly, I am not," thought the man, "so it must be my office for which I am not fit! That would be queer enough, but never give oneself away!"

Therefore, he praised the stuff he did not see, and assured them of his joy about the beautiful colors and the exquisite design. "Yes, it is really most charming," said he to the Emperor. Everyone in the town spoke of the magnificent stuff. Now the Emperor wanted to see it himself while it was still on the loom. With a host of selected men, including the two loyal officials who had been there previously, he went to the two artful impostors, who were weaving now with all their might, but without any strand or thread.

"Why, is that not splendid?" said both the honest officials. "May it please Your Majesty to have a look at the design and the colors?" And then they pointed to the empty loom, for each believed the other could doubtless see the cloth.

"What?" thought the Emperor. "I see nothing at all. This is indeed frightful. Am I stupid? Am I not fit to be Emperor? This would be the worst that could ever befall me!"

"Oh, it is very nice!" said he. "It meets with my highest approval."

Nodding contentedly and inspecting the empty loom, he did not want to confess that he could see nothing. The whole group he had with him gazed and gazed but did not see anything more than all the others.

However, just like the Emperor, each said in turn: "Oh, that is fine!" And then they advised him to wear the new magnificent robes for the first time at the Great Festival.

"It is magnificent, pretty, excellent," went from mouth to mouth, and everybody seemed to be delighted with it. Each of the impostors was awarded an order of knighthood to be worn in their buttonholes, and the title of "Court Weaver."

The swindlers sat up all night long till the morning on which the feast was to take place, and they had lighted sixteen candles, so the people could see how hard they were working to get ready the Emperor's new clothes. They feigned to take the stuff from the loom, cut it out in the air with big scissors, they sewed with needles without any thread, saying at last: "Look here, now the robes are ready!"

The Emperor with all his illustrious officials went himself to both the impostors who raised up one arm just as though they were holding something, and said: "Look, these here are the trousers! This is the coat. That is the shirt," and so on. "It is as light as a spider's web. One might think one had nothing on the body, but that is the very beauty of it!"

"Yes," said all the dignitaries, but they could not see anything, because there was nothing to see.

"Will Your Imperial Majesty condescend to take off your clothes." said the swindlers, "then we may put on the new ones here in front of the large mirror!"

The Emperor took off his clothes, and the impostors feigned to dress him in one garment of the new robes after the other, which were allegedly finished, and the Emperor turned round and round in front of the mirror.

"Ah, how well they suit, how perfectly they fit," said all. "What a design, what colors! These are showy robes!"

"Outside they are standing with the canopy that is to be carried over Your Majesty," announced the Grandmaster of Ceremonies.

"Well, I am ready," said the Emperor.

"Don't the clothes fit well?" and turned himself round again in front of the mirror, for he wanted to make believe as if he were examining his new robes closely.

The chamberlains who were entitled to carry the Emperor's train, bowed down so as to lift up from the floor with their hands. They strode along, and behaved as though they held something in the air. They dared not let it out that they could not see anything.

Thus, the Emperor strode about under the gorgeous canopy, and all people in the street called out: "How matchless the Emperor's new robes are! What a train he has to his robe! And how close it fits!" No one would let it appear that he saw nothing else, for he would have been deemed unfit for his post, or very stupid. No other clothes of the Emperor had brought about so much happiness as these ones.

"But he has nothing on!" said a little child at last.

"Hark! Listen to the voices of the innocent," said the father. And one person whispered to the next one what the child had said.

"He has nothing on at all!" at last shouted all the people.

That stirred the Emperor's mind, for the people to be right, but he thought to himself: "Now I must stand the test." And the chamberlains walked on, carrying the train, which did not exist at all!

GOLDILOCKS AND THE THREE BEARS

Once upon a time, there were Three Bears who lived together in a house of their own in a wood. One of them was a Little Small Wee Bear, and one was a Middle-sized Bear, and the other was a Great Huge Bear. They had each a pot for their porridge — a little pot for the Little Small Wee Bear, and a middle-sized pot for the Middle-sized Bear, and a great pot for the Great Huge Bear. And they had each a chair to sit in — a little chair for the Little Small Wee Bear, and a middle-sized chair for the Middle-sized Bear, and a great chair for the Great Huge Bear. And they had each a bed to sleep in — a little bed for the Little Small Wee Bear, and a middle-sized bed for the Middle-sized Bear, and a great bed for the Great Huge Bear.

One day, after they had made the porridge for their breakfast and poured it into their porridge-pots, they walked out into the wood while the porridge was cooling, that they might not burn their mouths by beginning too soon to eat it. And while they were walking, a little girl named Goldilocks came to the house. She had never seen the little house before, and it was such a strange little house that she forgot all the things her mother had told her about being polite: first she looked in at the window, and then she peeped in at the keyhole; and seeing nobody in the house, she lifted the latch. The door was not fastened, because the Bears were good Bears who did nobody any harm and never suspected that anybody would harm them. So Goldilocks opened the door and went in; and well pleased she was when she saw the porridge on

the table. If Goldilocks had remembered what her mother had told her, she would have waited till the Bears came home, and then, perhaps, they would have asked her to breakfast; for they were good Bears — a little rough, as the manner of Bears is, but for all that very good-natured and hospitable.

But Goldilocks forgot, and set about helping herself.

So first she tasted the porridge of the Great Huge Bear, and that was too hot. And then she tasted the porridge of the Middle-sized Bear, and that was too cold. And then she went to the porridge of the Little Small Wee Bear, and tasted that. It was neither too hot nor too cold, but just right. She liked it so well that she ate it all up.

Then Goldilocks sat down in the chair of the Great Huge Bear, and that was too hard for her. And then she sat down in the chair of the Middle-sized Bear, and that was too soft for her. And then she sat down in the chair of the Little Small Wee Bear, and that was neither too hard nor too soft, but just right. So she seated herself in it, and there she sat till the bottom of the chair came out, and down she came upon the ground.

Then Goldilocks went upstairs into the bed-chamber in which the Three Bears slept. And first she lay down upon the bed of the Great Huge Bear, but that was too high at the head for her. And next she lay down upon the bed of the Middle-sized Bear, and that was too high at the foot for her. And then she lay down upon the bed of the Little Small Wee Bear, and that was neither too high at the head nor at the foot, but just right. So she covered herself up comfortably, and lay there till she fell fast asleep.

By this time, the Three Bears thought their porridge would be cool enough, so they came home to breakfast. Now Goldilocks had left the spoon of the Great Huge Bear standing in his porridge.

"Somebody has been at my porridge!"

said the Great Huge Bear in his great, rough, gruff voice. And when the Middle-sized Bear looked at his, he saw that the spoon was standing in it, too.

"Somebody has been at my porridge!"

said the Middle-sized Bear in his middle-sized voice. Then the Little Small Wee Bear looked at his, and there was the spoon in the porridge-pot, but the porridge was all gone.

"Somebody has been at my porridge and has eaten it all up!"

said the Little Small Wee Bear, in his little, small, wee voice.

Upon this, the Three Bears, seeing that someone had entered their house and eaten up the Little Small Wee Bear's breakfast, began to look about them. Now Goldilocks had not put the hard cushion straight when she rose from the chair of the Great Huge Bear.

"Somebody has been sitting in my chair!"

said the Great Huge Bear, in his great, rough, gruff voice.

And Goldilocks had squatted down the soft cushion of the Middle-sized Bear.

"Somebody has been sitting in my chair!"

said the Middle-sized Bear, in his middle-sized voice. And you know what Goldilocks had done to the third chair.

"Somebody has been sitting in my chair and has sat the bottom out of it!"

said the Little Small Wee Bear, in his little, small, wee voice. Then the Three Bears thought it necessary that they should make further search; so they went upstairs into their bed-chamber. Now Goldilocks had pulled the pillow of the Great Huge Bear out of its place.

"Somebody has been lying in my bed!"

said the Great Huge Bear, in his great, gruff voice.

And Goldilocks had pulled the bolster of the Middle-sized Bear out of its place.

"Somebody has been lying in my bed!"

said the Middle-sized Bear, in his middle-sized voice. And when the Little Small Wee Bear came to look at his bed, there was the bolster in its place, and the pillow in its place upon the bolster, and upon the pillow was the shining, yellow hair of little Goldilocks!

"Somebody has been lying in my bed… and here she is!"

said the Little Small Wee Bear, in his little, small, wee voice.

Goldilocks had heard in her sleep the great, rough, gruff voice of the Great Huge Bear, but she was so fast asleep that it was no more to her than the roaring of wind or the rumbling of thunder. And she had heard the middle-sized voice of the Middle-sized Bear, but it was only as if she had heard someone speaking in a dream. But when she heard the little, small, wee voice of the Little Small Wee Bear, it was so sharp, and so shrill, that it awakened her at once. Up she started, and when she saw the Three Bears on one side of the bed, she tumbled herself out at the other and ran to the window. Now the window was open, because the Bears, like good, tidy Bears as they were, always opened their bed-chamber window when they got up in the morning.

Out little Goldilocks jumped, and ran away home to her mother, as fast as ever she could!

THE LITTLE PINK ROSE

nce there was a little pink Rosebud, and she lived down in a little dark house under the ground. One day she was sitting there all by herself, and it was very still. Suddenly, she heard a little tap, tap, tap, at the door.

"Who is there?" she said.

"It's the Rain, and I want to come in," said a soft, sad, little voice.

"No, you can't come in," the little Rosebud said. By and by she heard another little tap, tap, tap, on the window pane.

"Who is there?" she said.

The same soft little voice answered, "It's the Rain, and I want to come in!"

"No, you can't come in," said the little Rosebud. Then it was very still for a long time. At last, there came a little rustling, whispering sound, all round the window: rustle, whisper, whisper.

"Who is there?" said the little Rosebud.

"It's the Sunshine," said a little, soft, cheery voice, "and I want to come in!"

"N — no," said the little pink rose, "you can't come in." And she sat still again.

Pretty soon, she heard the sweet little rustling noise at the key-hole.

"Who is there?" she said.

"It's the Sunshine," said the cheery little voice, "and I want to come in, I want to come in!"

"No, no," said the little pink rose, "you cannot come in."

By and by, as she sat so still, she heard tap, tap, tap, and rustle, whisper, rustle, all up and down the window pane, and on the door, and at the key-hole.

"Who is there?" she said.

"It's the Rain, and the Sun, the Rain and the Sun," said two little voices, together, "and we want to come in! We want to come in! We want to come in!"

"Dear, dear," said the little Rosebud, "if there are two of you, I s'pose I shall have to let you in."

So she opened the door a little, wee crack, and they came in. And one took one of her little hands, and the other took her other little hand, and they ran, ran, ran with her, right up to the top of the ground. Then they said,

"Poke your head through!"

So she poked her head through; and she was in the midst of a beautiful garden. It was springtime, and all the other flowers had their heads poked through; and she was the prettiest little pink rose in the whole garden!

THE PRINCESS
AND THE PEA

There was once a Prince who wished to marry a Princess, but then she must be a real Princess. He traveled all over the world in hopes of finding such a lady, but there was always something wrong. Princesses he found in plenty, but whether they were real Princesses it was impossible for him to decide. One thing after another seemed to him not quite right about the ladies. At last, he returned to his palace quite downcast, because he wished so much to have a real Princess for his wife.

One evening, a dreadful storm arose. There was thunder and lightening, and the rain poured down from the sky in torrents. All at once, there was heard a violent knocking at the door, and the old King, the Prince's father, went out himself to open it.

It was a Princess who was standing outside the door. What with the rain and the wind, she was in a sad condition. The water trickled down from her hair, and her clothes clung to her body. She said she was a real Princess.

"Ah! We shall soon see about that!"

thought the old Queen-mother. Saying not a word of what she was going to do, she went quietly into the bedroom, took all the bed-clothes off the bed, and put three little peas on the bedstead. She then laid twenty mattresses one upon another over the three peas, and put twenty feather beds over the mattresses.

Upon this bed the Princess was to pass the night.

The next morning she was asked how she had slept.

"Oh! Very badly indeed!" she replied.

"I have scarcely closed my eyes the whole night through. I do not know what was in my bed, but I had something hard under me, and am black and blue all over. It has hurt me so much!"

Now it was plain that the lady must be a real Princess, since she had been able to feel the three little peas through the twenty mattresses and twenty feather beds. None but a real Princess could have had such a delicate sense of feeling.

The Prince accordingly made her his wife, being now convinced that he had found a real Princess. The three peas were, however, put into the cabinet of curiosities where they are still to be seen, provided they are not lost. Wasn't this a lady of real delicacy?

15

HANS IN LUCK

FROM THE BROTHERS GRIMM

Some men are born to good luck. All they do or try to do comes right—all that falls to them is so much gain—all their geese are swans—all their cards are trumps—toss them which way you will, they will always, like a cat, land upon their legs, and only move on so much the faster. The world may very likely not always think of them as they think of themselves, but what care they for the world? What can it know about the matter?

One of these lucky beings was young Hans. Seven long years he had worked hard for his master.

At last he said, "Master, my time is up. I must go home and see my poor mother once more, so pray pay me my wages and let me go."

And the master said,
"You have been a faithful and good servant,
Hans, so your pay shall be handsome."
Then he gave him a lump of silver
as big as his head.

Hans took out his pocket-handkerchief, put the piece of silver into it, threw it over his shoulder, and jogged off on his road homewards.

As he went lazily on, dragging one foot after another, a man came in sight, trotting gaily along on a capital horse.

"Ah!" said Hans aloud, "what a fine thing it is to ride on horseback! There he sits as easy and happy as if he was at home, in the chair by his fireside; he trips against no stones, saves shoe-leather, and gets on he hardly knows how."

Hans did not speak so softly, but the horseman heard it all and said, "Well, friend, why do you go on foot then?"

"Ah!" said he, "I have this load to carry, to be sure it is silver. But it is so heavy that I can't hold up my head, and you must know it hurts my shoulder sadly."

"What do you say of making an exchange?" said the horseman. "I will give you my horse, and you shall give me the silver, which will save you a great deal of trouble in carrying such a heavy load about with you."

"With all my heart," said Hans, "but as you are so kind to me, I must tell you one thing—you will have a weary task to draw that silver about with you."

However, the horseman got off, took the silver, helped Hans up, gave him the bridle into one hand and the whip into the other, and said, "When you want to go very fast, smack your lips loudly together, and cry "Jip!"

Hans was delighted as he sat on the horse, drew himself up, squared his elbows, turned out his toes, cracked his whip, and rode merrily off, one minute whistling a merry tune, and another singing,

"No care and no sorrow,
A fig for the morrow!
We'll laugh and be merry,
Sing neigh down derry!"

After a time, he thought he should like to go a little faster, so he smacked his lips and cried "Jip!" Away went the horse full gallop, and before Hans knew what he was about, he was thrown off and lay on his back by the road-side. His horse would have ran off, if a shepherd who was coming by, driving a cow, had not stopped it.

Hans soon came to himself and got upon his legs again, sadly vexed, and said to the shepherd, "This riding is no joke, when a man has the luck to get upon a beast like this that stumbles and flings him off as if it would break his neck. However, I'm off now once for all. I like your cow now a great deal better than this smart beast that played me this trick. One can walk along at one's leisure behind that cow—keep good company, and have milk, butter, and cheese, every day, into the bargain. What would I give to have such a prize!"

"Well," said the shepherd, "if you are so fond of her, I will change my cow for your horse. I like to do good to my neighbors, even though I lose by it myself."

"Done!" said Hans, merrily. "What a noble heart that good man has!" thought he.

Then the shepherd jumped upon the horse, wished Hans and the cow good morning, and away he rode.

Hans brushed his coat, wiped his face and hands, rested awhile, and then drove off his cow quietly, and thought his bargain a very lucky one.

"If I have only a piece of bread (and I certainly shall always be able to get that), I can, whenever I like, eat my butter and cheese with it. And when I am thirsty I can milk my cow and drink the milk. And what can I wish for more?"

When he came to an inn, he halted, ate up all his bread, and gave away his last penny for a glass of ale. When he had rested himself, he set off again, driving his cow towards his mother's village. But the heat grew greater as soon as noon came on, till at last, as he found himself on a wide heath that would take him more than an hour to cross, he began to be so hot and parched that his tongue clave to the roof of his mouth.

"I can find a cure for this," thought he. "Now I will milk my cow and quench my thirst." So he tied her to the stump of a tree and held his cap to milk into, but not a drop was to be had. Who would have thought that this cow, which was to bring him milk and butter and cheese, was all that time utterly dry? Hans had not thought of looking to that.

While he was trying his luck in milking and managing the matter very clumsily, the uneasy beast began to think him very troublesome, and at last gave him such a kick on the head as knocked him down. And there he lay a long while senseless.

Luckily, a butcher soon came by, driving a pig in a wheelbarrow. "What is the matter with you, my man?" said the butcher, as he helped him up.

Hans told him what had happened, how he was dry and wanted to milk his cow, but found the cow was dry, too.

Then the butcher gave him a flask of ale, saying, "There, drink and refresh yourself. Your cow will give you no milk. Don't you see she is an old beast, good for nothing but the slaughter-house?"

"Alas, alas!" said Hans, "Who would have thought it? What a shame to take my horse, and give me only a dry cow! If I kill her, what will she be good for? I hate cow-beef. It is not tender enough for me. If it were a pig now—like that fat gentleman you are driving along at his ease—one could do something with it. It would at any rate make sausages."

"Well," said the butcher, "I don't like to say no when one is asked to do a kind, neighborly thing. To please you I will change, and give you my fine fat pig for the cow."

"Heaven reward you for your kindness and self-denial!" said Hans, as he gave the butcher the cow, and taking the pig off the wheel-barrow, drove it away.

So on he jogged, and all seemed now to go right with him. He had met with some misfortunes, to be sure, but he was now well repaid for all. How could it be otherwise with such a traveling companion as he had at last got?

The next man he met was a countryman carrying a fine white goose. The countryman stopped to ask what was the time of day which led to further chat. Hans told him all his luck, how he had so many good bargains, and how all the world went gay and smiling with him.

The countryman then began to tell his tale, and said he was going to take the goose to a christening. "Feel," said he, "how heavy it is, and yet it is only eight weeks old. Whoever roasts and eats it will find plenty of fat upon it. It has lived so well!"

"You're right," said Hans, as he weighed it in his hand, "but if you talk of fat, my pig is no trifle."

Meantime, the countryman began to look grave and shook his head. "Hark ye!" said he. "My worthy friend, you seem a good sort of fellow, so I can't help doing you a kind turn. Your pig may get you into a scrape. In the village I just came from, the squire has had a pig stolen out of his sty. I was dreadfully afraid when I saw you that you had got the squire's pig. If you have, and they catch you, it will be a bad job for you. The least they will do will be to throw you into the horse-pond. Can you swim?"

Poor Hans was sadly frightened. "Good man," cried he, "pray get me out of this scrape. I know nothing of where the pig was either bred or born, but he may have been the squire's for all I can tell. You know this country better than I do. Take my pig and give me the goose."

"I ought to have something into the bargain," said the countryman. "Give a fat goose for a pig, indeed! 'Tis not everyone would do so much for you as that. However, I will not be hard upon you, as you are in trouble."

Then he drove off the pig by a side path, while Hans went on the way homewards free from care. "After all," thought he, "that chap is pretty well taken in. I don't care whose pig it is, but wherever it came from it has been a very good friend to me. I have much the best of the bargain. First there will be a capital roast, then the fat will find me in goose-grease for six months, and then there are all the beautiful white feathers. I will put them into my pillow, and then I am sure I shall sleep soundly without rocking. How happy my mother will be! Talk of a pig, indeed! Give me a fine fat goose."

As he came to the next village, he saw a scissor-grinder with his wheel, working and singing,

"O'er hill and O'er dale,
So happy I roam.
Work light and live well,
All the world is my home;
Then who so blythe,
So merry as I?"

Hans stood looking on for awhile and at last said, "You must be well off, master grinder! You seem so happy at your work."

"Yes," said the other. "Mine is a golden trade. A good grinder never puts his hand into his pocket without finding money in it. But where did you get that beautiful goose?"

"I did not buy it, I gave a pig for it."

"And where did you get the pig?"

"I gave a cow for it."

"And the cow?"

"I gave a horse for it."

"And the horse?"

"I gave a lump of silver as big as my head for it."

"And the silver?"

"Oh! I worked hard for that seven long years."

"You have done well in the world," said the grinder. "Now if you could find money in your pocket whenever you put your hand in it, your fortune would be made."

"Very true. But how is that to be managed?"

"How? Why, you must turn grinder like myself," said the other. "You only want a grindstone. The rest will come of itself. Here is one that is but little the worse for wear. I would not ask more than the value of your goose for it—will you buy?"

"How can you ask?" said Hans. "I should be the happiest man in the world if I could have money whenever I put my hand in my pocket. What could I want more? There's the goose."

"Now," said the grinder, as he gave him a common rough stone that lay by his side, "this is a most capital stone. Do but work it well enough, and you can make an old nail cut with it."

Hans took the stone, and went his way with a light heart. His eyes sparkled for joy, and he said to himself, "Surely I must have been born in a lucky hour. Everything I could want or wish for comes of itself. People are so kind. They seem really to think I do them a favor in letting them make me rich, and giving me good bargains."

Meantime, he began to be tired, and hungry, too, for he had given away his last penny in his joy at getting the cow.

At last he could go no farther, for the stone tired him sadly, and he dragged himself to the side of a river that he might take a drink of water and rest awhile. So he laid the stone carefully by his side on the bank, but as he sat down to drink, he forgot it, pushed it a little, and down it rolled into the stream.

For awhile he watched it sinking in the deep clear water, then sprang up and danced for joy, and again fell upon his knees and thanked Heaven, with tears in his eyes, for its kindness in taking away his only plague – the ugly heavy stone.

"How happy am I!" cried he. "Nobody was ever so lucky as I."

Then up he got with a light heart, free from all his troubles, and walked on till he reached his mother's house, and told her how very easy the road to good luck was.

THE WALRUS AND THE CARPENTER

BY LEWIS CARROLL

The sun was shining on the sea,
 Shining with all his might:
He did his very best to make
 The billows smooth and bright –
And this was odd, because it was
 The middle of the night.
The moon was shining sulkily,
 Because she thought the sun
Had got no business to be there
 After the day was done –
"It's very rude of him," she said,
 "To come and spoil the fun!"
The sea was wet as wet could be,
 The sands were dry as dry.
You could not see a cloud, because
 No cloud was in the sky:
No birds were flying overhead –
 There were no birds to fly.
The Walrus and the Carpenter
 Were walking close at hand:
They wept like anything to see
 Such quantities of sand:

"If this were only cleared away,"
 They said, "it would be grand."
"If seven maids with seven mops
 Swept it for half a year,
Do you suppose," the Walrus said,
 "That they could get it clear?"
"I doubt it," said the Carpenter,
 And shed a bitter tear.
"O Oysters, come and walk with us!"
 The Walrus did beseech.
"A pleasant walk, a pleasant talk,
 Along the briny beach:
We cannot do with more than four,
 To give a hand to each."
The eldest Oyster looked at him,
 But never a word he said:
The eldest Oyster winked his eye,
 And shook his heavy head –
Meaning to say he did not choose
 To leave the oyster-bed.
Out four young Oysters hurried up.
 All eager for the treat:

Their coats were brushed, their faces
  washed,
  Their shoes were clean and neat —
And this was odd, because, you know,
  They hadn't any feet.
Four other Oysters followed them,
  And yet another four;
And thick and fast they came at last,
  And more, and more, and more —
All hopping through the frothy waves,
  And scrambling to the shore.
The Walrus and the Carpenter
  Walked on a mile or so,
And then they rested on a rock
  Conveniently low:
And all the little Oysters stood
  And waited in a row.
"The time has come," the Walrus said,
  "To talk of many things:
Of shoes — and ships — and sealing wax
— Of cabbages — and kings —
And why the sea is boiling hot —
  And whether pigs have wings."
"But wait a bit," the Oysters cried,
  "Before we have our chat;
For some of us are out of breath,
  And all of us are fat!"
"No hurry!" said the Carpenter.
  They thanked him much for that.
"A loaf of bread," the Walrus said,
  "Is what we chiefly need:
Pepper and vinegar besides
  Are very good indeed —
Now, if you're ready, Oysters dear,
  We can begin to feed."
"But not on us!" the Oysters cried,
  Turning a little blue.
"After such kindness, that would be
  A dismal thing to do!"
"The night is fine," the Walrus said,

"Do you admire the view?"
"It was so kind of you to come!
  And you are very nice!"
The Carpenter said nothing but
  "Cut us another slice —
I wish you were not quite so deaf —
  I've had to ask you twice!"
"It seems a shame," the Walrus said,
  "To play them such a trick.
After we've brought them out so far,
  And made them trot so quick!"
The Carpenter said nothing but
  "The butter's spread too thick!"
"I weep for you," the Walrus said:
  "I deeply sympathize."
With sobs and tears he sorted out
  Those of the largest size,
Holding his pocket-handkerchief
  Before his streaming eyes.
"O Oysters," said the Carpenter,
  "You've had a pleasant run!
Shall we be trotting home again?"
  But answer came there none —
And this was scarcely odd, because
  They'd eaten every one.

THE OWL AND THE PUSSYCAT

BY EDWARD LEAR

The Owl and the Pussycat went to sea,
In a beautiful pea green boat.
They took some honey, and plenty of money,
Wrapped up in a five pound note.
The Owl looked up to the stars above,
And sang to a small guitar,
"O lovely Pussy! O Pussy my love,
What a beautiful Pussy you are,
You are, you are!
What a beautiful Pussy you are!"

Pussy said to the Owl, "You elegant fowl!
How charmingly sweet you sing!
O let us be married! Too long we have tarried:
But what shall we do for a ring?"
They sailed away, for a year and a day,
To the land where the Bong-tree grows.
And there in a wood a Piggy-wig stood,
With a ring at the end of his nose,
His nose, his nose,
With a ring at the end of his nose.

"Dear pig, are you willing to sell for one shilling your ring?"
Said the Piggy, "I will."
So they took it away, and were married next day,
By the Turkey who lives on the hill.
They dined on mince, and slices of quince,
Which they ate with a runcible spoon;
And hand in hand, on the edge of the sand,
They danced by the light of the moon,
The moon, the moon,
They danced by the light of the moon.

BED IN SUMMER

In winter I get up at night
And dress by yellow candle-light.
In summer quite the other way,
I have to go to bed by day.

I have to go to bed and see
The birds still hopping on the tree,
Or hear the grown-up people's feet
Still going past me in the street.

And does it not seem hard to you,
When all the sky is clear and blue,
And I should like so much to play,
To have to go to bed by day?